"Wake up, SPLASH . . .

... come PLAY

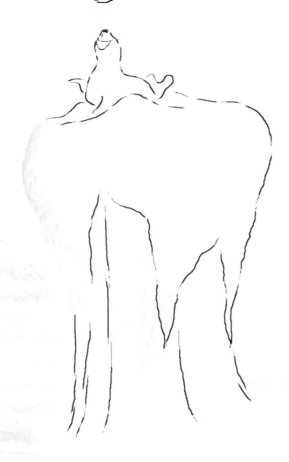

before the sun
rises and
melts the snow!"

SPLA

A LITTLE BOOK ABOUT

SH!

BOUNCING BACK

Written and Illustrated by MARIA VAN LIESHOUT

Designed by MOLLY LEACH

FEIWEL AND FRIENDS NEW YORK

SPLASH groaned,
"Leave me ALONE,"
just as a pile of snow fell,

PLOP

on top of him.

"Let's go SWIMMING, SPLASH!"

SPLASH looked down into the

deep, icy water.

He sighed, "I don't feel like . . .

...getting wet."

"I'll race you to the ICEBERG!"

SPLASH let out a DEEP sigh.

"Okay," he moaned. "I'll try. . . ."

SPLASH paddled as fast as he could,

but the current was faster.

HAHAHAHAHAHAHAHAHAHAHAHAHA

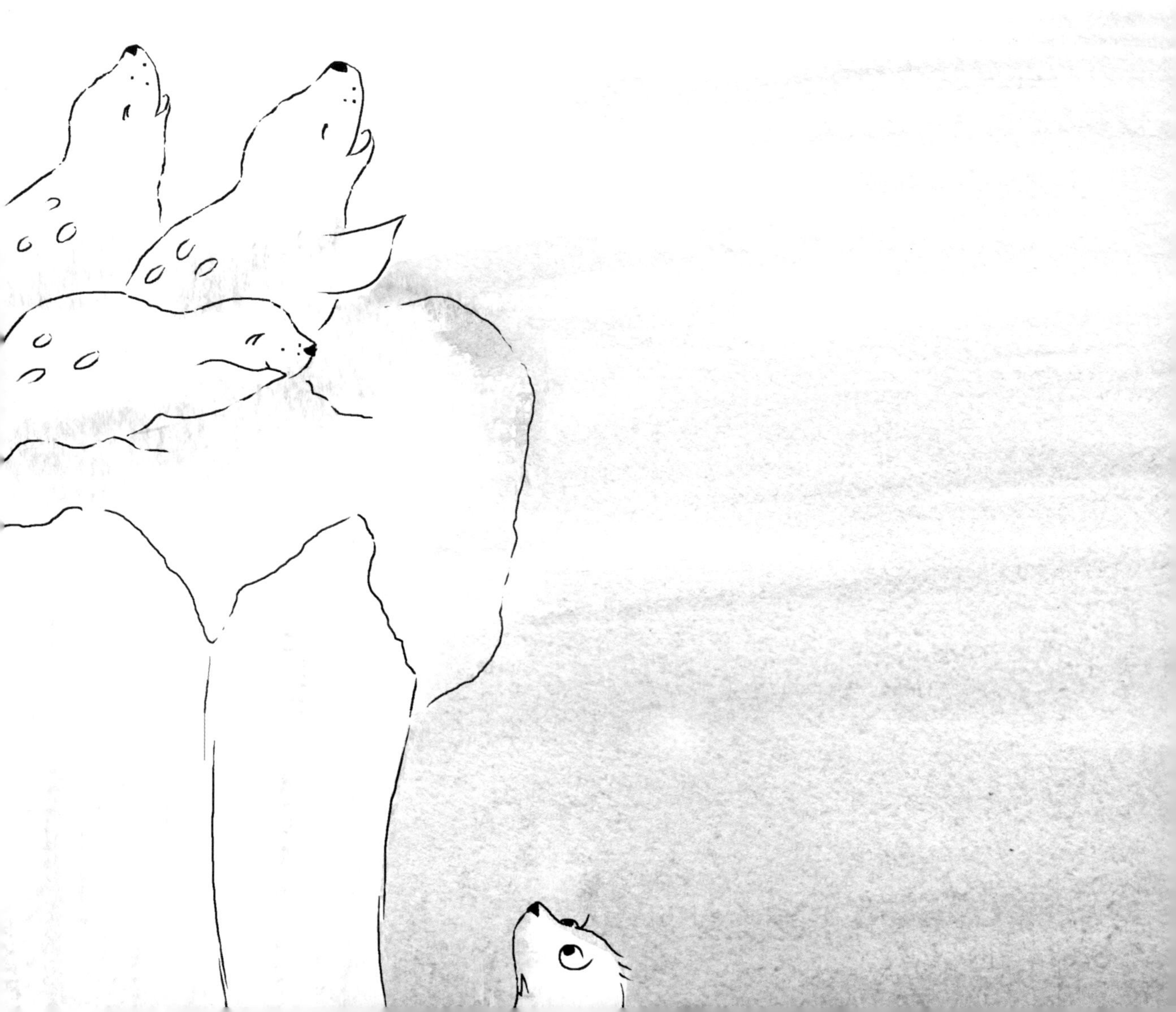

"Don't bother

rising today, sun," SPLASH sobbed.

The sun didn't rise.
It floated toward SPLASH, instead.

"OH, NO," he whispered.
"I've brought the sun down."

"I'm sorry.

Can I lift you back up?"

SPLASH tried to help the sun rise.
But it came back to him.

The HIGHER he pushed it into the sky,
the FASTER it came back.

AGAIN . . .

. . . and AGAIN.

With every bounce . . .

BOING
BOING
BOING
BOING   BOING   BOI
BOING   BOING
BOING

the sun shined a bit brighter.

BOING
BOING
BOING
BOING
BOING
BOING
BOING
BOIN·

And SPLASH did, too.

SPLASH beamed,
   "The sun is up . . . .

NOV 20 2008